A *Chip Off* The **Old** **Block**

A *Chip Off* The **Old** **Block**

Lloyd Antypowich

Library of Congress Control Number: 2013918677
ISBN: Hardcover   978-1-4931-1732-1
                Softcover   978-1-4931-1731-4
                Ebook   978-1-4931-1733-8

This is an actual story and tribute to my daughter, Cherie Jackson. The whole book is about her and I wrote it as a tribute to her.

This book was printed in the United States of America.

Rev. date: 10/18/2013

To order additional copies of this book, contact:
Xlibris LLC
1-888-795-4274
www.Xlibris.com
Orders@Xlibris.com
121925

To my family—Cherie's siblings, Cindy and Murray, and especially her mother; her daughter, Jennifer, and husband, Ty; her son, Jason, and his wife, Sarah; and the love of her life, Stuart.

Look for other books published by Lloyd Antypowich

A Hunting We Did Go

Lloyd is an avid hunter, loves the mountains, and has great knowledge of animals in the wilderness. This book makes the reader feel like he is along on the journey with him, experiencing the beauty of nature and the thrill of the hunt, as well as the acceptance of being outwitted by the animal he is stalking. Time and again, people have said, "I felt like I was right there with you."

Moccasins to Cowboy Boots

This is the journey of the author's life as he followed his dream to become a rancher. Filled with history and humor, his journey takes him from the homestead where he was born in the northern wilderness of Saskatchewan to Northern Alberta, where his family logged and owned a sawmill. Later he worked in the oil fields and road construction then became a farmer at Stettler, Alberta, and a miner at Elkford, British Columbia. But his dream carried him into the South Cariboo, where he bought a ranch at Horsefly, British Columbia, and became a logger to help support his dream. This is not a diary of his life; it is a humorous and determined journey of a man who refused to accept the concept of being unable to achieve any goal.

Louisiana Man

This is a fictional book inspired by a man the author spent an afternoon with while he was in his late teens. This man had lived a remarkable life and was happy to share his harrowing life stories, as well as showing off the spots on his back where buckshot still lay under the skin. The hero of this story, Tom Menzer, is the author's reincarnation of this sort of a man. Tom Menzer leaves his home in Louisiana to follow his dream. This is a story in the best of historical Western tradition, filled with drama, insight into the Indian culture in the late 1800s, the role of the white man as they pushed them aside, the struggles of a man who had a foot in both camps, and his journey into Canada to avoid the conflict. It is a tale well worth your read!

Horns and Hair of the High Country

This is a fictional collection of stories, based on the perspective of Elk, Bear, Goat, Sheep, and Caribou. These are all wilderness animals, and the book portrays how as they might feel as they associate with and are confronted by humans. This fictional book is drawn upon the author's intimate experience with the animals of the wild, portrayed through his vivid imagination and his great storytelling skills. It will be enjoyed by those who know animals, those who are curious, and the young people as well.

Cherie, the little trailblazer, riding in the mountains. When she is in this kind of environment, she just simply bubbles over with love, life, and that inner strength that she seems to draw from places like these. There are times when you will hear her say it's time for another trip into the mountains, and she will come back with her cup running over, willing to share it with everyone. Picture courtesy of Susan Kaeppel.

ACKNOWLEDGMENTS

To all the people who helped Cherie build the character that she has and for all the support that they gave her when she needed it the most. To Susan Kaeppel, for taking so many of those good pictures. And to Joyce Antypowich, who also was a good shot with a camera. And to the 120 pounds of dynamite that Cherie is.

Because I am just s'pposed to, I love you so much.

"Stop, let's understand each other. If you come one step further and have any intentions of harming me or my little camp, I will have to kill you." She was talking to two grizzly bears that were threatening her little spike camp over six thousand feet up on a mountain in the alpine. You might ask yourself, "What was she doing away up there, and how did she get there?" Read on, and you will learn the kind of person she is and what drives her vessel.

CHAPTER 1

From when man first set foot on this planet, he became an explorer, and we read all through history of all the places he has traveled and the things he has done, and that woman was to be his helpmate; some were leaders, and some were followers. And what makes some of us leaders? Well, I'm not sure. But to be a leader, it takes a strong-minded person, full of courage and fearless of the unknown. The men and women that have gone ahead and blazed a trail that others could follow have made this country what it is today. And what a great country it is, and I am very grateful to be living in it. We read of those who have walked over mountains—across valleys forested with timber as thick as the hair on a dog's back—crossed rivers, and traveled up and down them from ocean to ocean. They have left us a trail to follow. And for those who crossed the oceans to tie this world together so we can know it as we do, it would be safe to say they were a people strong and courageous and fearless of the unknown.

There are leaders and guides of many descriptions—political, religious, health, science, architectural, mechanical, and so many more—that it would take a book to list them all. The guide and outfitter is numbered among them, and if you don't think so, just try and tell that to a hunter from Germany, Sweden, or even the USA. And before these guides can take these hunters up into the mountains, there has to be a trail for them to follow. There are rivers to cross, swamps to go around, and campsites and cabins to be built in order to give that person a true wilderness experience and still be as comfortable as possible.

As we journey through life, we leave a trail for others to follow, but like all trails, they soon become washed out with time, and before long, they are forgotten. So I am going to try and help you follow and remember this little trailblazer. When the leaves have all fallen off the tree, it is hard to remember just what the tree really looked like, so this is for her kids and grandkids so they will be able to look back and know that their mother was one who blazed trails throughout the wilds of British Columbia.

The trail I am talking about started on January 27, 1964. Cherie was just a little sprout, four pounds eleven ounces, but soon, all concerns were put to rest because she was the feistiest little bundle of life you could imagine. When you go pick her up, she would get so excited she would kick all her blankets off, and her little legs and arms would go like she was a wind-up toy. We watched that little sprout grow into a beautiful flower.

As she matured, she chose the path that led her into the mountains and valleys of the beautiful British Columbia. One would wonder what inspired her, having been born a flatlander, to develop such a love for the mountains. But that she truly did, and it is so deeply embedded in her that I am sure she would be like a fish out of water if you were to take her from it. She is truly an outdoor person and has built her life around and within Mother Nature. Horses, foals, dogs, cats, cows, and calves are her first love, along with all the other animals and birds of the forest. When she relaxes, she will pick up her guitar and play and sing songs about packtrains up in the mountains, the valleys, the trees, and nature. Yes, she is truly like a flower.

The beautiful flower that blooms from the inside out.

The fragrance that she leaves behind is so pleasant to all her friends and family that it is a pleasure to be near her. She meets life every day with such a positive attitude that she is a real inspiration to the rest of us. Cherie operates her vessel in a different way than most of us, and even as a little girl in her preschool years, she had a mind-set that she lived by.

In her young life when she was just nicely able to express herself, she had that positive attitude, and when you asked her or told her something to do, she would say, "Well, because you are just 'post to." She could mimic birds and animals to a tee. It just came natural to her. Although she was always tiny, her size never stopped her from doing what she wanted to do. She loved horses and was always trying to associate herself with them. She spent many hours by herself brushing and trimming her horse. She would go over and over a lesson with her horse until it understood her. Her horses learned to have trust and faith in her that she would not make them do anything that would hurt them. She simply loved them, and they loved her. She learned to understand their language, and they learned to listen and understand her. Most of all, she had patience and never got in a hurry. If it took a little longer for them to understand her, that was OK with her. When she got done, there was a perfect bonding.

One Sunday afternoon, our family was having a lazy afternoon when in drove my sister and her husband with their four children. As we sat around and talked about the crops and weather and life in general, our kids thought this would be a good day to get even with the rooster that had been giving them a rough time. Now that they had more help, all those kids converged on that poor old rooster, and when they finally played him out after chasing him all over the farm, they caught him. They took him into the hayloft of the barn and threw him out the hayloft's door. He was a heavy-meat bird, so he didn't do too well at flying. When he hit the ground, it knocked the senses out of him, but he was still alive, so they got a short piece of two-by-four and put his head under it. Then they all stood on it. Well, that old rooster didn't know it was about to meet his demise, and they were finally going to get even with him for all the times that he had chased and pecked them.

When they thought they had him done in, the thought came to them that, just maybe, Dad would not approve of the treatment that they gave that old rooster. They took him out and tried to bury him in the manure pile behind the barn. The next day, I was doing chores around the barn, and here came this old rooster trying to walk across the barnyard. He would go a few steps then fall over, lie there for a while then struggle to get up and go a little farther, then fall over again and lie there. It looked like this old bird had some kind of a serious brain problem because his balance was a little of a canter.

So I asked the kids if they knew what happened to the rooster. At first, they were like little church mice, and no one said a word. Then Cherie said, "You know, Dad, he may have a brain problem."

"Oh," I said, "what makes you think that?"

"Well, yesterday after we stood on his head, he didn't look too good." That was when they told me what they had done to the old bird.

Cherie was about four then and said, "Dad, he wasn't 'posta be so mean to us."

I felt sorry for Cindy because she was the oldest and thought that they were going to be in trouble for beating up on the old bird. As they were all gathered around me, each one trying to tell me how they were justified for doing what they had done to the old rooster for all the times he simply terrified them, I could tell that in their little minds, this rooster was a much bigger problem for them than I had realized. As we all knelt around that old rooster and said a prayer for him, I promised them that I would take care of the old rooster and that he would never bother them anymore.

On the farm, the kids came with me almost everywhere that it was safe to take them. I was so proud to have them with me, and they learned about the birds and bees at an early age. I tried to explain to them how it all happened. They saw all the animals on the farm, and when they didn't understand some things, they would come to Dad to figure it out. When I purchased a new Hampshire boar to breed to the young York Landrace gilts, I asked the kids to tell me when Blackie was breeding the gilts.

One day when my wife, Gloria, had some ladies over for tea, Cherie came running into the house bearing the good news: "Yep, we are going to be having some little pigs, and some will look just like Blackie, and some will be all white because Blackie was breeding those gilts. He was, Mom, honest." And she was quite explicit. Yes, that was our little girl that should have been a little boy. Gloria was a bit embarrassed, but the ladies, being all farm gals, got a real laugh from the way she explained herself. They saw little calves, pigs, and foals all being born, and they knew that when I was inseminating a cow, there was going to be a little calf born nine months later. There was no magical thing about it. That was how it was, and I did not see why they should be told some fairy tale about the stork or something like that to only have to learn different later on. To have done differently would have made a liar out of me, so they were told up front the way things really were. By the time they went to school, they had a pretty good understanding of animal reproduction. It was kind of a sad day when we had to leave the farm because it was such a great place to raise four little kids.

After we had left the farm and were living at Elkford, British Columbia, in the Elk Valley trailer park, Gloria again had some ladies over for tea. The kids were out in the yard trying to make a new sandbox, and Cherie came running into the trailer. In her little hand, which was made into a fist, she said to Gloria, "Mommy, guess what I found? A pregnant earthworm!" Yes, the little girl could tell it like it really was. Maybe that is why she could look a grizzly bear in the eye and tell him to bugger off when he was threatening her spike camp.

When she was a young teenager, she was very feisty, and to her, boys were something to beat up on, and she would. If she couldn't beat up on them, she would get them on her horse and give them such a wild ride that would scare the living daylights out of them. I remember one day when some of these young roosters came over to ride horses, Cherie told this young guy to get on her horse with her and that she would give him a ride down to the barn.

It had been raining that morning, and the ground was quite slippery. The house was a thousand feet from the barn; there was a wooden gate to open as you went into the barnyard. When I saw him get on her horse, I just stood there to watch the excitement, knowing he was going to be in for a ride of his life. She took off down that lane to the barn as fast as her horse could go, and when she was twenty feet from the gate, she put her horse into a slide and slid right up to the gate. That young guy was about to crap himself because he thought they were going to run right into that gate. I could hear Cherie laughing her head off; she had just found her equalizer and had gotten even with him for some comment he had made about her horse earlier. When I got to the barn, I asked him how he liked his ride. All he said was that she was one crazy driver.

She was always trying to teach her horse or dog how to do some little thing differently. She could connect with animals, and as a result, they would do things for her that they would not do for anyone else. She had a lot of patience and also had a soft hand when working with the animals.

One day when we were living on the Black Creek Ranch and she was a young teenager, she asked me if I would take her to Horsefly as she wanted to see her boyfriend. I told her that I couldn't because I was too busy. The next day, as soon as all their chores were done, she and Murray, her younger brother, had two horses saddled, and they packed a lunch and rode eight miles across the country to see her boyfriend. She would get her visit and be back for supper.

Cherie and her older sister, Cindy, along with some of her other girlfriends, would ride their horses into the lake and dive off them. Horses were a big part of their growing-up years, and they could do almost anything with them and got a lot of enjoyment out of riding. They were a big help to me on the ranch at calving time or branding, and they were always there, willing to help whenever they could.

When she married Darcy Jackson, it wasn't long before they had a small string of horses and were going up into the mountains on trial rides. When the kids came along, they learned to ride, and they would go up into the mountains with her and Darcy. They would teach them all about horses and the outback. By the time they were ten years old, they had seen more country than a lot of prospectors, and they were just as familiar with horses as old cowboys. They have learned to respect the wilds but are not afraid of it and will jump at the first chance they can get to go on a trail ride up into the mountains. To sleep out under the stars on some mountain and cook a meal over an open fire is the highlight of their vacation. They have grown up to be respectable, accountable, and dependable young adults.

Not long ago, I was talking with a seasoned old rancher about branding calves out in the Chilcotin Country, west of Williams

Lake, and mentioned a gal that I thought was quite tough. He just looked at me and said, "The toughest gal I have ever saw is that Jennifer Jackson." I just smiled and wanted to say, "Cherie don't raise no riffraff." I have watched Jen flank a calf, sit on it, and call for the branding iron and say, "Don't take all day about it."

Cherie and Darcy had taught her very well, and when she entered 4-H in horse and dog classes, she breezed through it, winning most of the events that she entered. Later when she was out of school, she helped her mother break horses to pack and ride. The two of them would take guests up to the alpine for viewings of snow and grizzly bears. She loved to drive a team of draft horses on a wagon or sleigh, and at the old-fashioned Christmas, it was quite often Jenifer in the driver's seat.

Cherie will tackle jobs that one would think are away too big for her, but she will go about them just a-whistling, and before you know it, she is through it. Life has not always been a piece of cake or a bed of roses for her, but she seems to have a source that she can draw strength and energy from that gets her through the tough times.

The expression on her face tells it all.

She knows the feel of pain after having a knee operated on to repair the damaged and torn cartilage from an accident when her horse fell with her. That face tells it all; about this time she will be drawing on all her inner strength to help her get through the next few days until they can get her to a doctor to have him check it out. Then she will have to go through the long wait until she can get in to have the operation that she needs. Would you believe that she bandaged it up, put a knee brace on, and hobbled around the lodge, doing far more than she should ever have been doing? Her blanket saddle and bridle that are beside her on the quad will be getting a rest for a few months. Yet she never shies away from hard, physical work, in spite of her size; she always wears a smile. She has tried to raise her children the same way too and, in my opinion, has done a very good job of it.

She loves the music of the outdoors and animals and would rather be out riding her horse, chasing cows or leading a pack string of horses off a mountain than going to town. By now you will be wondering who this person is; she is my daughter, Cherie. She lives with Stuart Maitland, and together, they run Eureka Peak Lodge and Outfitters. They also are partners with Josh, Ty, and Jen on the Barker Creek Farms.

Cherie and Stu in a moment of relaxation.

A number of years back, Horsefly held a rodeo, and they were looking for young females to run for stamped queen. Quite a few people encouraged Cherie to enter, so she did. They had to ride their horses through a bit of a drill in order to qualify, then they had to do a public speak-off. Her topic was the tent caterpillars that Horsefly had been plagued with at the time. She completely turned a negative situation into a positive one when she told the judges that—believe it or not—she had found something good about them, and that is that they didn't bite us. She told them why we should all look for the positive things in life. She said it would put a smile on your face and a skip in your step, which is what you see when you look at her. When the judges made their decision, she got the nod. Her 4-H public speaking had come to the top for her. And I was so proud of her—as I had led that club for seven years, she was one of my 4-H students, and it was so good to see someone use their past teachings to their advantage.

Cherie Jackson was Horsefly's first stamped queen.

While Cherie was doing the drill with her horse, her little eight-year-old daughter, Jen, was riding Tess, a three-year-old quarter horse right in her mother's hoofprints. And yes, Jen grew up to be an excellent rider and horse trainer. She not only rode herd over the 130 head of cows for themselves, but she and her fiancé, Ty, rode herd for Ed Monical on another 200 head. They also calved out all their own cows and made all the hay to winter their cattle and horses. So I guess it is safe to say her mom didn't raise any riffraff.

Cherie (and Darcy Jackson's) daughter, Jen, doctoring a weanling calf. She managed the SPCA in Williams Lake for several years and, in doing that, got a lot of experience in animal health.

CHAPTER 2

One of the rough times in Cherie's life came when she and her husband went their separate ways. It was not easy to see the hurt that it caused all of them, but Cherie had reached a crossroad in her life. It was hard for the rest of us, but none of us knew just how hard it was for her. She made that decision and got on with her life. And like always, some criticized her, and some supported her. But one thing for certain, she knew that if it was to be, it was going to be up to her. So she rolled up her sleeves and started building a new life.

Tim and Dina Stephenson, guide and outfitters in Horsefly, offered her a job to cook for their hunters across Quesnel Lake, so she took it as she was such an outdoors person and loved the mountains. She could take a group of people up a mountain for seven days, do the wrangling and cooking, and come back as excited as if she had been on a vacation. Dina had just had a baby so was not able to stay in a hunting camp.

The base camp consisted of a tent frame and one small cabin. The kitchen tent was on a wooden platform and was equipped with a propane kitchen stove sink shelving a table and a cot. That was to be her home for the next six weeks. There was no running water, except when she was running to the creek with a bucket. The shower was a solar one, and that suited her just fine. She was in for the adventure.

When she met them at the docks on Quesnel Lake, the guide, Wolf Ditzel, and Dina were arguing in German about taking Cherie along with him. He said, "What the hell I am going to do when I need to pack into a goat camp, take a girl along for company?"

Dina said that Cherie was more than capable to handle that and that she was really good with horses. He asked, "What is this, some superwoman?" Dina said, "Just trust me, she can handle the job." Her first group of hunters would be hunting for black bears. They were from Germany—Otto and Inga, a very nice older couple. Inga stayed in camp with her most days. She didn't speak much English at all, but actions are universal, and Cherie learned a few words in German, so they struggled through the language barrier.

Cherie taught Inga how to make pine-needle baskets to help pass the time. She spent a lot of time splitting wood. Those big round blocks were a real challenge for her with an axe. She did not have a splitting maul. She baked bread, lemon pie, and cookies and, of course, cooked the main meals. She also looked after the horses, and as they were grazing in the cut blocks, she would check to see that they didn't go too far from camp and that all the bells were still on.

After the bear hunt was over, there was a week before the next hunt, and Tim said that they would all go home and come back when the next hunters came. Cherie did not like the idea of leaving the horses there unattended. She had her own horse out there, and she had no intention of leaving him there without her, so she volunteered to stay behind to look after the camp and the horses. Tim thought it would be good to have someone in the camp so the bears didn't come and wreck it, but he did not want to leave Cherie there by herself. She firmly maintained that if her horse stayed, she would be staying with it.

Cherie said the week went by slowly, but she had lots to read and spent a lot of time in the cut blocks with the horses. She also spent a lot of time working on a quad trail from the main logging road to the camp along the lakeshore. She would take the quad and a small trailer and haul gravel to fill all the ruts that were in the road. Some of them were quite deep as the ground had never been graded into a road. When it rained, the vehicles would sink in the ground and leave these deep ruts that nearly made it imposable to get through with a truck. It took a lot of gravel and many trips to get that road to where you could drive over it and not get stuck.

One day, her good friends, Pam and Bill Webb, brought Jennifer and Jason out to see her. It was a welcome break from the solitude of the wilderness camp. They came across the lake in their own boat; it was an outing for them but a special surprise for Cherie. The kids ran up and down the shore looking for special little stones and driftwood and really enjoyed themselves.

Wolf came back with the new hunters to the camp on the shore of the north arm of Quesnel Lake, which was only accessible by boat and twenty-five miles from the nearest lodge. She got right to cooking the meals and making lunches for the hunters. She would go for a pail of water and would see these big grizzly tracks in the sand. They had been made sometimes during the night. But they did not seem to bother her little camp.

When Wolf had gotten the black bears for the hunters, it was time to go up the mountain for goats. To get to where the goats were was going to take the hunters up to the top of the mountain. Cherie said she would take the guide and the hunters up the mountain if they helped set up the spike camp. Then she would take care of the rest while the guide and the hunters looked for their goat. She was as excited as a child with a new toy; she had never been in that part of the country before and couldn't wait to explore it.

Tim had only one pack horse, which was actually a saddle horse that he had borrowed from someone in Alberta. This horse had never been packed before, and the first attempt at packing ended in a rodeo and with stuff scattered all over the place. However, they did manage to get her packed again, and off they went. Wolf didn't like horses too much, so he walked and led the pack horse while the hunters and Cherie rode on the other horses. That trip took her up a mountain to a timberline at six thousand feet. There the guide helped make the spike camp.

After, she took them farther up the mountain and across a very treacherous slide then dropped the guide and the hunters off and returned to the spike camp. When she got back to where the slide was, she said it looked a lot worse going down than it had when they were going up. It was more than two thousand feet over the edge, and let me tell you, that is no cakewalk. A few guides have lost horses over that edge. She said she was glad that there was no frost on the trail, so she took the dally off her saddle so if any of the horses slipped, they would not pull her horse over the edge.

When she got back to the spike camp, she unsaddled the horses, rubbed them down, and then hobbled them so they could graze on the alpine grass while she put up the electric fence that would keep the horses in during the night. Then she built a fire pit, gathered some wood for her fire, and cooked herself some supper. While she ate, she was admiring the beautiful sunset. From her camp, she could see the east arm of Quesnel Lake, Wasco Lake, and the numerous cut blocks that had been made by the logging companies; she was literally on top of the world.

She prepared herself a mattress of boughs, and she was ready for a good, long sleep. In the morning, the air was quite crisp; there even was a little frost, but the promises of a beautiful day was in the making, and from six thousand feet above the valley floor, the view was breathtaking. As the sun rose higher into the sky, all the south slopes were warming up quite quickly.

After breakfast and a few cups of coffee, she was ready for whatever the day would bring. She found some nice big flat rocks and improved on the fire pit. Then she went back to where she had found the flat rocks and found one that would make a good tabletop. It was too big to carry, so she pushed, rolled, and slid that rock until she had it right near the fire pit. Then she maneuvered it onto some bigger rocks and had the makings of a pretty good-looking table.

She was a bit tuckered after wrestling with that rock, so she had a coffee and sat there and enjoyed the scenery. Then she made a makeshift outhouse. She used rocks and whittled a pole for a seat. She said it faced overlooking the valley, and voila, she had an outhouse with the most amazing view.

She knew Wolf and the two hunters might be back that night. She took out her journal and thought it would be a good time to catch up on it. As she came out of the tent, she stopped to look at the beautiful scenery once more. It was then that she saw the two grizzly bears. They were still quite a ways from her camp, so she sat down with her gun and camera at her side and proceeded to write in her journal.

When she looked up again, there were the two grizzly bears not a hundred yards away, sitting and looking at her camp. She thought, *Oh great*. She got her gun and went into the horse fence. This was the first time she had seen a grizzly bear so close. She took some pictures, but the grizzly bears kept coming closer. She shouted at them and told them to go away, but they just kept coming closer. Then she fired a shot at them. That is when they both stood up on their hind legs and looked at her. They got down on all fours and kept coming her way.

She lit a fire, hoping that the smoke would scare them off. When they were less than fifty yards away, she knew she could be in trouble, so she fired a shot right beside one. That stopped them for a while.

One went to where the bullet hit the ground. He scratched around and sniffed the ground. He apparently never had experienced what a bullet could do to him if it was carefully aimed at a vital spot on his body. He sat down while the other one came right to the fence. The horses were snorting and blowing. Cherie told me that she had made up her mind that if that bear was going to take one step inside that fence, she was going to start shooting. She said she didn't know if she could kill him, but she said she was not going to stop shooting until he was dead or she was out of shells. She reloaded her gun to make sure she had all the firepower she could get. She thought that if she could hit him in the spine, that would disable him.

Now she had a plan, so she waited. That bear came and put his nose on the electrified wire not thirty yards from her and, of course, got himself a good shock. She said he jumped back and slapped at his head and roared and growled and had a bit of a tantrum. Then she yelled at him, but he still refused to leave so she fired another shot right in front of him. That got his attention. Possibly some fragment of rock and bullet might have tickled him a wee bit, and he ran off, taking his friend with him.

She said her heart was beating so fast that she stayed inside that electric fence for a while before she felt it was safe and that they were actually gone. Later she needed some water but wasn't sure that they had totally left the area, so she hopped on one of the horses bareback to go for the water. On the way back, the horse got a little too close to the fence and touched the wire, and it took off with her holding on to the halter rope in one hand and the coffee pot in the other hand.

She said, "I hit the dirt and decided that was enough excitement for one day, so I went and had a nap." Before she went to bed, she tied one horse at each end of the tent. She knew that if the bears were to come back later that night, the horses would warn her. The night was calm, and she said she slept like a baby.

The next day, she went for a walk. She was looking at the lake, and away down below her, there were fishing boats on the lake, but they were so far away that they never even knew she was up there. Then she heard a noise below her, and it was a wolf. She didn't have her camera with her, so she went to get it from her tent. When she got back, the wolf was gone.

She went back to the camp and started baking a cake in a frying pan as she had no oven. She greased the pan, poured the batter in, and placed a large metal bowl over as a lid, and hey, it turned out great. She turned the heat to low, and it never even burned. When the guys got in that night, they sat down to a big pot of stew, a freshly baked cake, and peaches—good enough to fill the leg of a hungry goat hunter.

When Wolf and the hunters came into camp that evening, he was really impressed with what she had done, and he was having second thoughts about his cook. She had a story to tell them. She made their supper, and after they sat around for a while looking at her pictures, one of the hunters said, "Cherie, weren't you scared when that bear was after you?"

She said, "Well, yes, I was, but I was not going to let him know that."

And that is what makes up my little 120 pounds of dynamite a true chip off the old block.

Wolf and the two hunters had not gotten their goat yet, so they were going to try an area closer to camp. That meant they would be using the spike camp for breakfast and supper and to sleep in. I think that made Wolf feel a little better about leaving Cherie in camp all by herself. That morning after she had made them a lunch, she wished them good luck and said, "Don't you guys worry about me. I will be just fine. Go and get yourself a nice big goat."

They did find a respectable goat, but the hunter was looking for one that was bigger and older, so he passed him up. She did up the breakfast dishes then took the horses to a spring for a drink and hobbled them so they could graze the high alpine grass. She was enjoying her morning coffee when she noticed a grizzly bear not more than two hundred yards from her camp. As she watched him, a second one came over the ridge.

She wondered if they were coming back to finish the job they had started yesterday. She realized what she had just done and said "Cancel, cancel" to get rid of that negative thought. As they started to come down the mountain toward her camp, she said, "I knew I had to stop them before they got any closer, and to be honest with you, I did not think my thirty-thirty was big enough. So I focused all my mental concentration toward them and sent them thoughts, telling them that they should not come any closer to my camp, that they should go and look for their mice, roots, and chipmunks somewhere else. 'I am not afraid of you, and if you try to hurt me, I will have to kill you.'" She sat there and just focused on them and, in her mind, kept thinking, *Stop, don't come another step closer.*

And guess what—they sat there and watched her and her little camp for quite a long time. Then they walked down the mountain in another direction. She said, "I just looked up, and I said, 'Thank you for helping me. I really don't know where you are, but I must be closer to you up here on this mountain, so thank you again. I really needed this one.'"

Could that be one of the reasons that she loves to go up the mountains? One thing for sure, she seems to get her batteries charged when she is out there. She is such a positive-thinking person and believes in the power of the subconscious mind and that all things happen for a reason. And it is her challenge to understand that reason. She understands the need to be cautious, and safety is always on her mind. Maybe that is what keeps her from getting into trouble.

CHAPTER 3

They finished the hunt on that mountain and then broke up that spike camp to head back to the base camp on the lake. Cherie said she had tears in her eyes when she had to leave that little camp behind because it had become so personal—her fire pit and table and her mattress were so comfortable; the scenery was second to none. Somehow the bears were secondary; one would have thought that she couldn't wait to get off that mountain.

When they got to the base camp, Tim was there with his big aluminum boat, the *Grizzly Spirit*. He picked the hunters up to take them back to the airport so they could fly back to Germany. By the end of her time working together with Wolf, he had a whole new opinion of her. When he and Tim dropped her off at home, he was trying to thank her for all her help, and Tim was teasing him about getting all sentimental. He said, "Well, you should see what she can do and how hard she worked. You wouldn't believe it." Tim just smiled and was probably remembering the conversation Wolf had with Dina on the docks at the beginning of the season.

I talked to Tim a little later on, and the first thing he said was "Did you hear about Cherie?" I guess a really concerned look came on my face, and Tim said, "Oh, everything is OK, but did you hear about the grizzly bears that came into her camp?" He told me that those German hunters were so impressed they had left her a really good tip. He also told me that if that had happened to some of his guides, they would have crapped themselves. Cherie just blows me away. Nothing seems to be too big of a challenge for her, and she is such a little thing. I don't believe she ever thinks of not being able to complete a project; she just goes ahead and figures a way how to get it done.

Tim took her back to Horsefly so she could have a few Mommy days with her kids before she went back across the lake. They did a few more moose hunts lower down the mountain and were successful on both accounts. Wolf had made a good hanging tree to keep the meat out of reach of the grizzly bears so they could not steal it. But they sure did leave lots of tracks around to show that they were there. When Tim's hunts were over, she was looking for work again.

Tim and Stuart were dealing on Tim's guiding area, and that is where Cherie met Stuart. After he bought Tim's area, Cherie went to work for him at Eureka Peak Lodge and Outfitters. It was so nice to have such good facilities to work in, but she hoped Stu would let her go up the mountains to cook for the hunters so she could sleep under the stars and enjoy that fresh mountain air.

It took a little while for Stu to really be convinced that she could do all the horse wrangling and packing. He taught her some of the diamond hitches, and that made packing that much better. But he wanted her to stay in the lodge more because she could cook and bake so well. The hunters were enjoying her fresh-baked bread, cookies, and cake, and just loved it. Stu knew that the best way to a man's heart and pocketbook was through his stomach, and Cherie was helping him out on this one. She made the clients feel very welcome.

She was doing well with the tips that they left her too, and she sure could use it. Stu got her a little bit of help, but for most of the time, she was nearly run off her feet. She always kept looking for ways to make things look better—a flower, a feather, or some trinkets helped to dress up the lodge. She was diligent at keeping the grass cut and putting out bird feeders and flowers to help attract the hummingbirds. She built beds for a small garden, and Stu helped her build a greenhouse, as the season is quite a bit shorter high up in the mountains. She came home to my ranch and got good, rich top soil to put in her flower beds and garden.

Soon the lodge was taking on a whole new look. But the workload was also getting bigger. In the summer holidays, her two kids, Jen and Jason, would come out and help, and she loved that.

Eureka Peak Lodge from the water on Gotchen Lake.

The lodge is situated on Gotchen Lake in the Caribou Mountains. It is built out of logs and consists of a kitchen, a pantry, a living room with a large rustic fireplace, a dining room that will sit twenty people, plus their living quarters upstairs. On the outside, there are two decks, the larger one facing the lake. There are two four-man cabins with a sitting deck facing the lake; they have full plumbing, power, and running water. Then there are two cabins that house two people; each one has all the amenities.

There is a power plant; a shop; a tack shed (which holds all the saddles and camping gear); a meat shed; a woodshed; a guide cabin that will house seven guides; a corral; a boat launch; a horseshoe pit; and a large yard that requires a lot of attention, especially with all the flowers that Cherie has planted. She also plants a garden that she loves to work in; the hunters just love when she cooks fresh veggies right out of the garden that the clients are forever raving about her cooking and baking.

The deck overlooking Gotchen Lake and all the baskets of pretty flowers.

More beautiful flowers all planted by the hand that knows how to give the lodge that homey feeling.

One year she was having a real problem with the Steller's jays. They were plucking out her bean plants as fast as they sprouted and pushed through the ground. She asked Stu to shoot at them to see if that would scare them away. He really was not too interested in shooting those pretty birds, so she begged him to bring his shotgun so she could take care of the situation herself. But he kept finding a way to put it off. One day I got the call. "I need you, Dad. Come and thin out some Steller's jays for me." She sounded so desperate I couldn't refuse her. After the job was done and she had picked up all the birds and feathers, her problem wasn't a problem anymore.

One day Stu asked her how she was making out with the birds. He said there didn't seem to be as many around anymore. She just looked up at him and said, "Honey, I just took care of that little problem, and things are just fine." She has been at Eureka Peak ever since, so I think it is safe to say that she has found not only a way to make her garden and flowers grow but love as well.

What does she do? Well, let's start with housekeeping; that is women's work. She's up at 5:00 a.m. to start the generator and make a big pot of coffee then make a breakfast of bacon and eggs, hash browns and toast, and jam and peanut butter; set the table; ring the breakfast bell; make the lunches; and do a few "honey dos" then kiss him good-bye. Now she will finally take time enough to have a coffee and a piece of toast.

As she sits there, she looks the situation over and decides what to do next.

She'll do the dishes and clean and tidy up the lodge then check and clean the cabins. Next, she'll water the flowers that she has planted all around the lodge plus the small garden she loves to work in. Later today might be a good day to cut the lawn. When that is all done, she'll go in and bake some bread and maybe a batch of cookies (the cookie jars are almost empty). Now while the bread is rising and the cookies are baking, she will make herself a sandwich and a cup of coffee.

The phone rings; it's Kathy, the bookkeeper from One Hundred Mile House. She tells Cherie there will be four hunters flying into Williams Lake airport the day after tomorrow. That means everything will have to be planned right to the minute; it's a three-hour one-way trip. Oh well, she'll do a little grocery-shopping at Great Canadian while she is in town; that will keep the pantry full.

While the cookies are baking, she starts prepping supper. She'll start out with a big moose roast rubbed down with some spices and lots of garlic, a big bowl of potatoes, some carrots, some green beans, and a salad. That should fill a leg or two, but man, those guys can sure eat when they come in from hunting. As she is setting the table, she wonders if they will get anything that day. It has been a bit slow because the weather has been so mild. If they do, they will have to get it to the abattoir in Horsefly really quick so the meat won't spoil.

The dogs, Rex and Rougher, are barking; she goes to the window to have a look—lo and behold, if it isn't the hunters and the guide from across Quesnel Lake. That means there will be three more hollow legs to fill for supper. Oh well, she will just cook another six spuds along with more carrots and beans. The guys will have to settle for ham sandwiches the next day, as there will not be enough of that big moose roast left over for lunch. The cookies are done just in time. Aye!

Joe, the guide, comes in. He is all smiles, so she knows they got their moose, but now, they want her to stop and listen while they tell her all about how they got it. She tells them to just keep talking; she really is listening to them, but there will be ten people for supper tonight, and she did not expect that.

When that fresh bread comes out of the oven, those hunters leave the cookie jar alone and beg her for some bread. She looks out the window; the dogs are running to the gate. Stu must be coming. She stops to watch a little longer, and sure enough, it is Stu, and he has a nice moose in the back of his truck. The horns are really impressive, and she knows they will really be bragging about that one. They are early, but they will go through their bragging session and have a few drinks, and by that time, she will have supper on the table.

One of the hunters comes and says to Cherie, "I sure am glad that I let you talk me into coming earlier. You know, Cherie, Stu called that moose from away down in the valley, right up to the back of the pickup. He was less than seventy yards from us when I shot him."

He is one happy hunter. The supper hour is noisy; everyone seems to have something to say, and they all want to say it at the same time.

After supper, Stu goes out and skins the moose out and hangs the meat in the meat shed. He will take it to the abattoir early in the morning. Cherie gathers the supper dishes, puts them in the dishwasher, does a little breakfast prepping, and is ready to call it a day. It is 9:00 p.m. The day after, she will do it all over again.

The next day, after all the breakfast excitement is over, she has her morning coffee as she sits in the sun on the deck of the lodge overlooking Gotchen Lake. She is thinking it will not be too long before this beauty passes and Mother Nature paints a new picture of a winter scene across the land. The loons with their friendly yodels will soon be gone for another year. Then Stu will start his trapline again, and there will be all the skinning and stretching of the fur. Sometimes he will get so many she will help him.

Christmas and New Year will soon be here, and Stu will open up the lodge for friends and family. That always is such a fun time. Everyone will come in on their sleds and leave their vehicles out on the main road, and some years, every cabin is full and all has a great time. There is always a lot to eat because everyone brings something, and Cherie will warm it all up in her kitchen. There will be dancing and singing, and a great time is had by all.

As she sits there with her eyes closed, she remembers all the good things that have happened in her life; then she is suddenly brought back to reality by the scream of a bald eagle that has caught a fish and is telling all that want to listen that he is not only a magnificent bird but a master fisherman as well.

Jeepers, she has kind of drifted off; she has to get the pack gear ready for Stu and for the hunters that are coming the next day. They are going to use a spike camp and try for goats and big mule deer bucks. Stu has told her which horses he is going to use so she can have the appropriate pack gear and camp equipment ready. She will load the groceries into the pack boxes on the morning that he will leave for the hunt.

When she finishes with the pack boxes, she comes back into the kitchen and notices that the cookie jars are almost empty again, so she decides she will bake enough to fill them this time. By then Stu should be back and she will need to have dinner ready for him and the hunters that he is taking to the airport.

After dinner, he tells her that he will take the hunters in to catch their plane, do the shopping, pick up the hunters who are arriving at the airport that afternoon, and bring them back to the lodge with him, and if she can bring the horses in for the next hunt. She heaves a sigh of relief and tells him he has a deal. She will far rather work with the horses than go to town.

And so goes each and every day until the last hunter that has booked a hunt with them has gotten his game. Then there is lots of work left to do, but they can do a lot of that together, and she likes that. The lodge has to be shut down for winter; all the water is drained so the pipes will not freeze, and the horses have to be hauled back to the ranch. Then they will live in the house in the Black Creek Valley, and that will make it easier for her to visit with her friends. And of course, it also makes it much easier to spend time with her kids. She will be able to get back to singing with her friends in a group called Harmony. She had Rich Kenny build her a new guitar and is anxious to get to playing it. Rich does an awesome job of making musical instruments.

Stu will bring the horses back on the barge from the hunting camps that are across Quesnel Lake as the *West Fraser* barge is making its last run for the season. And then it is time to start trapping. Stu does a few trapping excursions where people go along with him on his trapline when the snow gets deep enough so he can use his snow machines. I have gone with him when we have traveled more than sixty miles.

For those New York and California folks, this is a trip of a lifetime, and I can just imagine the bullsh—ing they will do when they get back home. But I guess that is OK because they have paid for it, so they can really lay it on. When there are wolverines or wolves in the traps, they can really get quite excited, but most of the fur-bearing animals are killed instantly because of the use of the conibear trap. Then there is all the skinning, fleshing, and stretching. Some of that Cherie has learned to do, like the martins, squirrels, and weasels. Each trapline client is given two pieces of fur to take home with them.

He also does a few cougar hunts, and then later while Stu is giving a few trapper courses, Cherie is busy putting together the newsletter that they send to all their clients to share all the happenings of last year's hunting.

By the end of January, they go to trade shows in the USA to promote their guiding business. They go to places like Reno, Vegas, Portland, and a few others. One thing for sure, their life is never boring. It is nearly impossible to tell you all the things she does and loves every minute of. So I think I will let her tell you in her own words of the places she has gone and some of the things she has done.

CHAPTER 4

Cherie, coming out of the mountains from cutting trail.
Notice her power saw—she knows how to use it too.

Cherie will be telling you about opening up trails, leading a string of pack horses into an area that very few people have ever been to, crossing creeks and swimming rivers with horses, and walking down game trails as they tie ribbons to mark the trail that will need to be cut wider so the horses with the pack boxes can bring in supplies and pack out the meat that the hunters will get. It will be on some of these trips that she will encounter bull moose in the rut and grizzly bears. Through her eyes, she has seen Mother Nature in its purest form that will take a lot of people several lifetimes, and then I don't think even then they will see what she has, and that is because she sees things differently than most of us.

Tyler, Cherie, and Jennifer coming back from a long, hard day of trail-cutting in the rain.

Cherie on her way into the Niagara to cut trail with Stuart. A lot of this area had never been opened up, so they could hunt it with horses. There were a few old trapper cabins that they hoped to find and make trails to. The hunting was of great promise, and hunters were eager to try out the new area, but first, a lot of hard, back-breaking work had to be done.

A Piece of Heaven
Cherie Jackson

As cook and hostess of the lodge, I don't get to spend much time out in the bush or up those beautiful mountains, so I guess what stands out in my mind this past year is our trip up the Niagara! For one reason or another, I have never been able to make it. This year was the year. And let me tell you, it was well worth the wait. On this particular trip, Stuart and I wanted to take the horses over and cut a trail into the Niagara valley from the Blue Lead Creek. I had been around the end of the east arm of Quesnel Lake on the horses four or five times but not for at least eight years, so the trail was a little foggy in my mind, but I was reasonably confident that I could find it. We loaded up the horses and trucked them for approximately two hours. That trip in itself is a beautiful one—it takes you down old logging roads past remote mountain lakes, and at one point, you are so high you can see Horsefly Lake and the east arm of Quesnel Lake at the same time. It is absolutely breathtaking. We finally reached our destination, which I think Stuart was a little unsure of as he questioned me several times to make sure it was the right spot.

We unloaded the horses, packed up, and headed out. The ride was as beautiful as I remembered it to be. It winds through the alpine, out into the open meadows with those little stunted trees and meandering creeks and those incredible snowcapped mountains as a backdrop. It is simply magical. We rode into Silvertip Lodge around five that evening with only one minor delay. No, we were not lost; we were just exploring, as I like to say. Stuart and I started cutting trail up and over the Niagara from the Blue Lead but realized that it would take a lot longer than we had time for. We really wanted to get up to the Niagara on this trip.

We left the horses at Silvertip Lodge, and Josh and Tyler picked us up in our boat, the *Grizzly Spirit*. From there, we headed to the head of the Niagara valley, where the falls pour into Quesnel Lake. The trail that we were cutting is between the glacier and the falls, and we crossed it many times. Sometimes the horses had to swim; other times it is only belly-deep—the river is only ten or twelve miles long and flows the length of the Niagara valley. It is very beautiful.

Niagara Falls on Quesnel Lake.

The boys and I cut our way up while Stu pushed on with the quad to the river and then started cutting back to us. Stu and I then left the boys cutting and clearing and headed up the river in the twelve-foot aluminum, just to take a peek and maybe find the dollhouse.

The Niagara River is a glacier-fed river, and it is therefore full of silt, so it appears gray in color. It actually kind of sparkles because of it, but when you scoop it up in your hands to drink, it looks OK. We put the boat in and headed up the river. It was so exciting; every corner was a new adventure with all the little creeks running into it, the sandbars, and the islands. We saw geese along the shores, beaver making their way out of the little runoffs, and lots of moose tracks along the riverbanks.

The glacier that feeds the Niagara River. The river is only ten or twelve miles long and feeds right off the glacier and any of the other watershed off those other high mountains.

As we rounded one corner, we saw what we had been waiting for—a majestic moose just standing there on a sandbar, wondering what the heck we were. He let us get quite close before he turned and ran into the river and swam out in front of us. I got some incredible pictures as he was climbing out of the water on the opposite shore.

As we worked our way farther up the river, we came to some large meadow on either side of the river, which were sheltered by large mountains. I stood up to get a better look into the meadows, and standing only fifty feet offshore was a magnificent bull moose. He just looked at us as we went by and went back to eating. I wonder how many more bulls we passed without even knowing it.

A nice bull moose right beside the river on their way up the dollhouse. The game just stood and watched when they came along. They seemed to have little fear of them, even the grizzly bears.

We got out of the boat to start cutting our way downriver. I turned and looked across to the opposite shore, and there stood a little moose all by itself. It seemed to appear from nowhere. We looked up and down the river, but its mom was nowhere in sight. We watched it while we ate lunch then started to cut trail again. He made his way down the river with us. About ten minutes into cutting, I turned back for another look, and here came Mom with another little one in tow. As she came closer, we saw that the calf had been in a tangle with something. Its ear was torn badly, and there was a lot of blood on its neck. The cow had obviously fought off whatever tried to harm her baby, but in doing so, she had signs of also being roughed up. They made their way past us and met up with the other one.

We continued our way through the incredible, tranquil valley, sometimes through open areas with large trees and moss;

other times it was willowy and thicker. We had never been to the dollhouse before, so we didn't know what to expect. We were able to follow an old trail made by Howard Lowry and crew back in the '60s and '70s. We were quite pleased to discover that the cabin was in quite good shape and respectable in size.

It was as well just the way you might imagine an old guide cabin to look. The roof was covered with thick moss with the occasional little fir tree growing out of it. There were old saws, shovels, axes, and horseshoe all hanging on the wall on the porch. Inside was even better. Below the four-by-four-foot window in the kitchen was a long table with wooden benches, a propane cookstove in the corner, and shelves lined with all the pots, pans, and plates you would ever need. There was also an old wood heater to dry all your wet cloths. There were three beds in the main area and a large bed in the back room, which also had buckets of provisions hanging from the roof. I absolutely loved it. We gave it a good sweep, and it was just like home.

We took the boys by boat up to the cabin the next day and spent the next three days cutting trail. To me there is something so incredibly magical about walking through the forest along the river on those old trails that you never know what awaits you around the next bend. I love clearing them out, making them passable for man and horse.

Stu and I made our way back up the river, past a set of waterfalls, trying to find another cabin that was farther up the valley. We crossed two slides and, I think, infringed on a couple of grizzly bears by the sound of it. We couldn't see them because of all the tall alder bush, but they let us know they were there. Our trail wound around obstacles, picking up parts of the old trail here and there, but the cabin was still nowhere in sight.

We knew we had at least three and a half hours to hike back to the dollhouse, so we reluctantly decided to head back. Just as we turned back around the first corner in the river, a cow and a calf were standing in the stream; it was a nice way to end our venture upriver that day.

The next day, Tyler and I took a stroll in the meadow just out in front of the cabin. We were standing on the riverbank, talking, and out walked this absolutely huge bull with not a care in the world. I couldn't believe it; he just stood there and looked at us for a while and then turned and walked back into the bush. Yes, there he was right in front of the cabin; it doesn't get much better than that. It was a sad day when we had to go home.

Tyler and I offered to come and spend the summer up there to finish all the trails. Well, we didn't get to spend the summer, but we did get to come back again, and each year was as peaceful yet exhilarating and full of beauty and adventurous as the last one. I look forward to spending more days up that magnificent valley next year.

Chapter 5

Trail-Cutting in the Niagara
Cherie Jackson

The plans were made; we were going to trail the horses around the east arm of Quesnel Lake and over the Blue Lead and down into the Niagara valley. We wanted to finish the trail from the dollhouse to the third cabin and as far as we could get, fixing up the undesirable spots along the trail as we went. We had been waiting for a call from Wally Vietch, the barge operator, to tell us he was making a run up the east arm, but time was running out, and we had trail to cut.

The barge is operated for the benefit of West Fraser Timber Co. Ltd. It is used to barge fuel and equipment across the lake to the logging contractors that deliver the logs to a dumping site, where they are put into large log booms and then pulled by the tugboat across the lake to a reload site. There they are taken out of the water and bucked into various lengths and put on trucks that will haul them to Williams Lake to the mill. So when the barge was going to make a run up the east arm of the lake, we were hoping to get the horses barged up to save a lot of time, instead of trailing them all the way around. Kerstin Kalbanter, a young vet student from Germany, and I were at the lodge around dinner time, and we asked her if she would like to accompany us on our adventure. She was more than willing, not really knowing what she was in for. Well, as plans do, they changed several times before the final plan was put into action. The call came from Wally that he was making run the next day, and we should have the horses there by 5:00 a.m. if we wanted to catch a ride on the barge with him.

So by 10:00 p.m., Kerstin, Dylan, and I were off to load horses and meet the barge. As we planned to leave early the next morning anyway, we had all the horses in the corral, so the loading went quite smoothly even though it was in the dark. We stopped at the Patenaude corrals and picked up my stallion, Cody, to take along, and we were off to meet the barge.

We arrived at the reload on Quesnel Lake by 5:00 a.m. Dylan helped us load the horses onto the barge before he headed to Hundred Mile House. Kerstin and I rode the barge up the lake with the horses. We did manage to get a few winks of sleep curled up in the cab of a big fuel truck that was headed to the logging camp. We arrived on the beach at the trail at the head of the Niagara valley around one thirty that afternoon.

We unloaded the horses and what gear we had bought with us onto the beach and waved good-bye to the barge crew. We thanked them for the ride and set out to make ourselves some lunch and get comfortable until Josh and Tyler arrived with the rest of the gear and supplies. They arrived with our boat, the *Grizzly Spirit*, at around three o'clock. We unloaded all the supplies and gear, and while we were packing our horses, they took the quad and headed up the trail to the riverboat on the Niagara River above the falls.

They were to go ahead and finish fixing the bridge that my son, Jason, and Brent had started earlier. As we were saddling up, my stallion, Cody, started showing signs of colic. So being that Kristin was a vet student, she kept him walking round and round in a circle and would not allow him to lie down and roll. Colic is very painful to a horse, and if they are allowed to lie down and roll, they can end up with a twisted gut.

Eventually, we seemed to work out the problem of his stomach, so we saddled him up and tailed all the rest of the pack horses together. It was four o'clock, and we were ready to head up the valley. It was a late start, but if everything went well, we could make it by seven or eight o'clock. Everything was going along nicely until we ran into the first big fir log that had been blown down across the trail. I had no saw with me as the trail had already been cleared out earlier. We made it around with only a small degree of difficulty, and off we went until we encountered the next piece of blowdown. I thought about turning back, but we were already three hours into the trail, and the guys were expecting us at the other end, so on we went. We managed to make our second river-crossing just before dark; I'm not sure what Kristin was thinking at this point. She had never ridden a horse in the wilderness, let alone across a fast-moving river so deep that the horses at some points were almost swimming.

Crossing the Niagara, Kristin was getting a real lesson on moving guide horses into the Niagara. Can you imagine the stories she had to tell her friends back in Germany? She should have made a good vet because she was one gutsy young girl.

Some things you know and take for granted, like lifting your legs up so you don't get soaked. Kristin was soaked right up to her waist, and there were times that the horses nearly had to swim, and when we were not in the river, the rain seemed to try and get the rest of us wet in spite of our rain gear. She was a good sport and never said a word though.

We rode for the next three and a half hours in the dark, me leading four pack horses. Thank God I did a good job of packing them and had Kristin taking up the rear to help keep everything going smoothly. We encountered several more areas with trees across the trail and, shall we say, had some interesting times trying to get the string of pack horses around them in the dark. I was really grateful for my trusty old Houdini as, at times, he knew the trail better than I. His night vision is a lot better than mine. We did have a few arguments as to who was right and wrong on a few occasions. In one particular spot when he wanted to head out into the river after we had already made a river-crossing, it turned out he was right. With all the rain we had, the water had come up, and the small channel we just popped over on foot when we cut the trail out was now one major channel. I can't imagine what Kristin was thinking as I argued back and forth with him trying to make him go farther up the trail that wasn't even there, until I got my flashlight and discovered that he was right and I was wrong.

The problem with the correct route was a rather large log that lay across the trail right where we entered into the water, so the horse had to jump over the log and land in the channel, and I had no way of knowing how deep it was. But it was the only way to go, so in we all went—well, except for Cody, who was the last in the pack string and, having shorter legs than the rest, got dragged over the log and ended up on his side in the water, but it didn't take him too long to right himself, so up we went the Niagara on our midnight run.

About an hour before we reached the cabin, there was a rather large creek that we had to cross. My dog, Rex, who was also on this grand adventure, kept getting swept across the creek and into the river. We were already across the creek with all the horses when he started barking and let me know that he could not make it. Then I heard the wolves howling, at least two, maybe three. As much as I hated to leave Rex, I decided to get the horses out of there in case they spooked in the dark. They were all tied together, and that might have been a little too much of an adventure, even for me. So we pushed on with heavy hearts, not knowing what would become of Rex.

The smell of woodsmoke and that twinkle from the lantern in the cabin was a welcoming sight. It was 11:30 p.m., and we were soaked to the bone and just a wee bit tired. We unloaded all the pack saddles from the horses and decided to go and look for Rex. Tyler grabbed his gun, and he and Kristin and I walked back to the creek to see if he was still there or if the wolves had gotten him. As we neared the creek, we could hear the wolves once again and thought for sure that Rex was a goner. Then over the rush of the water, we could hear him barking, and Tyler waded through the creek and carried Rex back across the creek. We all headed back to the cabin for some dry clothes and a good night's sleep.

The next day dawned with the sound of rain on the roof, but we didn't care. Our clothes were mostly dry, and after all, that's the way it goes when you are cutting trail up the Niagara.

After a hearty breakfast, we headed up the river on the horses. There were a few spots that needed cutting and a few alternate routes that needed to be sought out. Our goal was to get to the third cabin and as far past it as we could in the next four days. The day went along quite smoothly as we made our way up the old trail that winds along the river, through the old growth forests and all the slides.

It was heaven, I tell you, just simply heaven. Then just before noon, our luck sure took a turn for the worse. As we were making our way through a small creek, the trail was right beside a big old fir tree, and Tyler's horse, Easter, caught his foot in it and stumbled and fell over on his side with Tyler still on him. We got Tyler out from under Easter, but the horse still had his foot stuck in the root and was now lying on his side in the creek and could not get up. We were worried that he would break his ankle if he struggled to get up.

I called to Josh to hurry and get the saw and cut the root before he started to struggle. It took several cuts to finally get Easter's ankle free. Easter still wouldn't get up, so we thought if we took the saddle off him, it might help. That turned out to be a little more difficult than we thought because he was lying on it. After practically disassembling the saddle and Josh pushing up on his neck and head, he finally got it out from under him. He immediately tried to get up and threw his head back and smacked Josh right in the jaw, sending him flying backward into the creek.

Once we had the saddle off him and his ankle free, he got up with only a little effort. We looked at his ankle; he could stand on it even though it was badly swollen, but it did not appear to be broken. Lucky for us one of the pack horses that we were not using that day followed us, so we took Tyler's rigging and put it on him and let Easter go free. We returned to the cabin that night and had ourselves a hearty meal then packed up everything and headed up the trail.

I'm sure Easter was as happy with our detour around the old tree as we were. We only had one minor incident that day, widening a part of the trail that ran along the river. We were all off the horses, and Houdini decided he wanted to pass the horse in front of him, and he fell into the river. It was about a five-foot drop; he went completely underwater. He swam his way up the river to an easier exit spot; he was fine, but my saddle and everything that hung on it was soaking wet.

It was a long day of trail-cutting, making our way through the big open meadows. With the clouds hanging low and those huge mountains looming up in the distance, we wound our way along the river and back up the timber where the trail was impassable, only to end up back down along the river and into more open meadows. We finally saw what we had been anticipating all along the way—the roof of the third cabin nestled in the trees on the point of the river with the white mountains in the distance. What an awesome site.

The cabin was incredible. With a little spit and polish, it would be a great place to camp. It is small but has all the comforts of home—a bunk with a foam mattress and a kitchen with all the pots, pans, dishes, and cutlery; a propane stove for cooking and two full propane bottles; a case of naphtha gas; packs; hammer; nails; lantern; and an old broom made from spruce boughs. In no time, we had it all cleaned out and reorganized. We tested it out that night and found only one small leak by the chimney of the wood stove.

The next day, we started out past the cabin to try and connect the trail that Stu and Brent started earlier by working their way from Christian Lake down to the third cabin, but time was running out, and we had to be back at the dollhouse that night. We did make it to the big meadow (as we call it), and even though it was raining and cloudy, we could tell that on a clear day, it would be even more impressive than it was now. There was a break in the clouds; we could get a glimpse of the glaciers at the head of the valley above Christian Lake. The meadow was absolutely huge and seemed to go on forever—everywhere you look, you could see big mountains surrounding and the Niagara River winding up the valley. The beauty of this country was simply amazing, but we were running out of time, so we took one last look at this magical, pristine piece of wilderness.

I said a little prayer in hopes of getting back here again soon, and we headed back down to the cabin to pack up and head down the valley to the dollhouse. That trip from the dollhouse to the beach was not without its excitement. As we were crossing one of our log bridges, one of the horses that was running free decided to try and pass the horse that I was leading and ended up on his back in the channel of water. We had quite a time trying to right him, as it was a narrow and about four feet deep, and to make matters worse, he had a saddle on that was now soaking wet.

He couldn't get his feet under him to roll over, so we ended up having to cut the bridge out so he could get on his side. Then we had to get the saddle off to get him up on his feet again. Once on his feet, he couldn't get out of the channel as it was just too deep for him. Finally, we turned him around, and Josh walked him up the channel. As I always say, everything happens for a reason! We found an even better crossing farther up the channel that didn't even require a bridge, so we made another alternate route.

In all the excitement of trying to get Turk out of the channel, none of us tied up our horses. We just bailed off and went to work, and you guessed it—the rest of the crew continued down the valley without us. We never even noticed that they were gone until we had Turk out. So Kristin and I made a mad dash down the trail in hopes of finding the horses before the river-crossing but got there just as they were reaching the other side. I can tell you this—that will never happen again. Tyler was drifting down the river in the boat, and we all managed to hitch a ride with him. There were only two inches of freeboard left as that boat was loaded to the gunnels.

We only had to go a short distance before we caught up with the horses and resumed our ride out without further incidents. I guess you could call us the guinea pigs although I prefer to call us the pioneers—the ones who went before you to make the way easier and safer. We do so with the greatest intent that as exciting as these adventures are for us, you never have to do them. The trail-cutting is a job I look forward to each year with great anticipation.

CHAPTER 6

An Opportunity of a Lifetime
Cherie Jackson

It all started last winter at the sportsman show when Jerry Martin and Steve Blankenship booked at ten-day moose/goat combo hunt up the Niagara. I was so excited listening to them planning the trip. Can you imagine what it would be like to travel that upper valley on horseback, knowing that no one had been there for thirty years? I could hardly believe my ears when Jerry said, "Cherie has to come along as our cook." That was sweet music to my ears, and no one had to ask me twice. The plan was to have someone pack the horses in ahead of time, and we would fly in a Beaver into Christian Lake, which is near the head of the valley.

Gideon, the pilot of the Beaver that flew us into Christian Lake—a master at his trade.

This may sound simple, but the fact is that the cutting of the trail had to be finished first. My son, Jason, and Dylan Spencer went in late July to scout out the trail that would let us go from the end of the pinfold valley up and over the pass to the Niagara. This would save us three days of riding and a six-hour barge trip up the east arm of Quesnel Lake with the horses. This route had been tried by a previous outfitter but was rumoured to be impassable because of a rock face. Dylan and Jason found a way. Mind you, it took a special string of pack horses to make it, but we happened to have just that kind of pack string. Dylan and Tyler Maitland went on another trail-cutting expedition, this time to finish the entire trail to Christian Lake. I wasn't able to make it on this trip, but I didn't mind because I knew I would be up there for ten glorious days later on. They started in the pinfold valley and pushed their way up and over the pass into the Niagara, then up the river until they reached the trail coming down from Christian Lake that Stu and Brent had started the year before.

It was finally finished! With the combined effort from all of us, the trail up the Niagara was finally opened. Oh, what memories it had given us over the last three years—some boat adventures, wet river-crossings, bear invasions, sinking of the horses into the river channels; you name it, we had experienced it all. A few days before the hunt started, Dylan and Tyler packed in eight horses and all the gear we needed for a good camp and a successful hunt. Before I knew it, Gideon had the Beaver docked at Gotchen Lake, and we were loading all the food and personal gear plus the four of us and my dog, Rex. I thought we would never get off the water. But Gideon, being the superb pilot that he is and the Beaver being, well, the Beaver, we had no problem at all. I had never flown in a floatplane before, so it was exciting for me and Rex as well. It was a wonderful sight to see Dylan and the horses on the shore of Christian Lake, one that hadn't been seen for over thirty years.

We unloaded all our gear and said good-bye to Gideon and packed up the horses and headed off into the direction of our camp. The first thing I noticed on the trail was the abundance of large blueberries and huckleberries. I could foresee fresh pancakes with blueberries and huckleberries mixed into the batter. I spent the next few days in camp getting firewood, picking berries, and looking after the horses. It felt good to just relax and read a book, go for a walk, or whatever, although I must admit I was pretty excited when Stu and Jerry came into camp and said they had gotten a big bull moose at the far end of the valley. I was able to go with them and help pack it out.

Stu and Jerry had told me how beautiful the upper valley was, but nothing could have prepared me for their astounding beauty that lay before me that day. Everywhere you looked was absolutely breathtaking. The valley must be three miles wide with the blue-and-green crystal-clear Niagara River winding through it; on either side, there are large meadows full of golden-colored grass, and there are game trails beaten out along it. Mountains on all sides offer such an array of beauty, from rock faces scattered with mountain goats to large alder slides with moose feeding on them. I like the mountains glistening in the sun and the huge glacier at the head of the valley.

It's awesome. Best of all was that feeling you get from knowing that only a handful of people in all the world had ever been there before you. We made our way up the valley, crossing the river at least seventeen times, each bend providing more beauty than the last one.

Crossing the river on a hunt up the Niagara valley, looking for a moose and a goat in one of Mother Nature's most beautiful pieces of handiwork.

I was overwhelmed. I must have taken 250 pictures that day. We finally made our way to the moose with only minor trail-cutting, and what a beauty he was—he came to rest in the middle of a big meadow at the base of one of those amazing mountains. Stu and Jerry got to work quartering and boning the moose, and I got the pack boxes ready. Before I knew it, their moose was in the boxes, the rack tied on, and we were off to camp. Now he could concentrate on his goat. He was one happy hunter.

A very happy hunter with his trophy moose. The goat would come next, and it did—a ten and a half incher. It is hunts like these that make repeat customers and others stand in line to get a piece of the same kind of action. What they don't realize is how much work goes into developing an area like this and how much expense there is in gearing up thirty horses and all the feed it takes to keep them. But after experiencing some of that good home cooking that Cherie can produce, they will be telling their friends and booking a hunt for the next year.

The trip back to camp was every bit as spectacular with all the fall colors and the sun shining on the mountains and the river. I got some excellent pictures. Just when I thought I could take no more, we rounded the corner in the river and were about to cross it when I spotted an animal. It wasn't a moose or a caribou, and it sure wasn't a deer. That only left one thing—an elk. We don't have them here, but there he was, larger than life. He stepped out, took a look, probably not believing what he was seeing either, then turned and disappeared into the bush. I can't believe it—I saw a bull elk in the Niagara valley. I wonder how long it will be before more of them move in or if that was a once-in-a-lifetime thing.

It was great to be back at camp that night, but I found myself wondering when I would be back there again. Jerry got his goat. Steve and Dylan spotted one up the valley and made the treacherous climb upward and got him. Before I knew it, Gideon was flying in with the Beaver to take Jerry and Steve and their goat and moose back to the lodge. Stu and I decided to stay a few more days to just scout out the valley for future hunts. Dylan left with the extra horses and gear and was going to call us when he reached that truck, to let us know he made it out OK.

Well, we got no call that night and none the next morning, so we saddled up and headed out to look for him. The ride down the valley was quite a bit more challenging than the upper section, but it had its own unique beauty. We got to the big meadow and made our way up the pass and over into the pinfold. I had never been that way before, so I was seeing something new all over again. The pass was . . . well, let's say it does take a special string of pack horses to make it over that rock ledge and down the other side. We made it through with no mishaps. The mishap came later. As my horse was trying to crawl over a moss-covered boulder, he slipped and fell on my leg. He jumped up and fell again, and I put my leg out to get off, and my knee popped. That was the end of the trip for me. Stu got me back on my horse, and I road for another two hours until we got to a logging road.

The truck was not there, of course, because Dylan had taken it. He did leave a message, but the phone lost signal. We caught a ride with one of the heli-loggers to our camp on Quesnel Lake, and I stayed there for the next few days while Tyler and Stu went back up the Niagara and broke camp. Would I do it again? You bet that I would.

I can't wait—that could not stop me. I get my knee fixed this January and will be ready to go again by next summer on more adventures of a lifetime.

CHAPTER 7

Wrangler Wrap
Cherie Jackson

Hi, everyone. Two thousand and six was a year of new projects and people around the lodge. We had the pleasure of Antje Kahlheber's company for a few months. Antji is from Germany and was here in Canada on vacation. She wanted to learn more about horses and taking them into the wilderness. We said, "Come on out. I am sure we can arrange something."

Yes! I welcomed having someone to help train horses. Antji turned out to be such an asset at the lodge; she had no fear when it came to horses and was willing to watch and learn. She is also a very hard worker and doesn't mind doing the least-desirable jobs either. The two of us would get all the chores done around the lodge and then spend the rest of the day working with the young horse. Together we trained two of our three-year-olds to ride and four of our two-year-olds to pack.

There were some exciting times, and the corral needed a few repairs, but we took all our trainees on the six-day pack trip through the mountains two weeks later and only had a few minor disagreements with them. All in all, they did really well, and we never got tossed, so that was a good thing. We weren't sure if Antji had enough of the wilderness yet, so we sent her on two back-to-back ten-day hunts in the Niagara valley.

She went along to help with the horses and cook. When she got back, he told me she simply loved it. She went exploring every day that she could and even had a bull moose follow her and her horse one day. We were really sorry to see her have to go and hope she might be able to come back again next season.

We had a few new projects this year. There is now a much-needed shop for all the tools and fishing gear at the lodge and then a new woodshed as well. Stu and I put in a new dock this spring, and plans for a new corral system are in the works. My son, Jason, and I went out and got eighty pine rails, and we bought a bundle of treated posts. But we ran out of time before the ground froze, so that project will have to wait until next spring.

I put in three new flower beds this spring and think I am finally finished with all that nonsense, but I think I might need a bigger potato patch. We will see how things go next spring.

This is Daddy speaking now. I do not know where she gets all that drive and energy from, but I can hardly believe that it all came from Gloria and me. I would love to go with her on some of those adventures, but I know I could never keep up with her. When I started teaching her to train and ride horses, I had no idea she would take off like a wildfire and do all the things that she does now. And you know what? I have a granddaughter that has followed right in her footsteps. Together they have taken eight and ten clients up the mountains and right into the alpine for a week, and during that time, they have encountered black bears, grizzly bears, wolverines, and those ever-protective cow moose.

Jen, her daughter, has gone through 4-H and did exceptionally well with horses and dogs. I somehow think that if Jen were to have kids, they would be born with spurs, cowboy boots, and straw hats. When I asked her about my great-grandkids, she brought me a puppy for Christmas, so I may have to wait for a long time.

Cherie and her daughter, Jennifer, with their two dogs,
giving them a cool-off dip in a really cool pond on one of
their guest trail rides.

When Jen and her friend were young teenagers, they would
come out to the ranch, and when some of the mares were due to
foal, they would sleep in the tack room of the barn so they could
witness the birth of the new foal. The mare only foals when she is
ready, and those kids would stay out in the barn and wait her out
until she finally foaled.

CHAPTER 8

Cherie loves to take people up the alpine on trial rides. She loves to sleep out under the stars and cook over an open fire. She just simply loves the mountains.

Cherie on her Appaloosa horse, along with her trusty old friend, Rex, leading a string of clients on a trail ride up the alpine. She will spend six or eight days riding all over Eureka Peak and down the bowl as well. Eureka bowl is an old volcano that has not been active for thousands of years. Picture courtesy of Susan Kaeppel.

Cherie relaxing by a mountain stream. Picture courtesy of Susan Kaeppel.

Cherie in the alpine admiring the flowers.

Cherie and Jen have done a lot of trail rides together, and among her most favorite would be guiding clients on the alpine rides up to Eureka Peak. Most of these rides are three-day rides, but some are five to seven. She really learned to pack from Stuart. He is a good teacher and really knows what he is doing.

"He taught me how to use a double diamond on a top pack, and that is what I do best," she says. "I have also learned how important it is to have a well-balanced pack. I think our first trip alone without anyone along to help us was about seven years ago." Jen and Cherie had been training horses all spring to ride and pack, and Stu had a group of people that wanted to go on a pack trip.

Out on a trail ride!

We wanted to go, but the horses were still green, so we gave the better riders some green horses, but most of them got seasoned horses. All the pack horses were green. When we got to where the trail needed cutting, I asked myself, *How did I get myself into a situation like this?* As long as the horses could keep going, they did a really good, but all that power-saw noise and trying to keep them standing still while the trail was cleared was a challenge.

Stu came along to the trailhead and helped them pack up the horses to get started. It took a while before they got the swing of it.

Cherie would get the green riding horses going, and then the two green pack horses would put the binders on and pull her to a stop. Her young riding horse soon learned how to pull pack horses. Jen was in the same predicament—just too many green horses.

When she had to cut some of the bigger trees, it could be a tricky business making sure it wasn't spring-loaded or going to roll down on you. She managed to do it—with confidence, she hoped—as the guy that was with her would offer a little help. But he never said a thing to her and never offered to help. He either didn't know how to do it himself or was not much of a man. Once the saw was back on the pack horse, they were off again; they made it to the camp without any other problems.

That was a good workout for those green horses, and they were content to just stand and let them take the packs off. They also enjoyed the rubdown that Jen gave them. Then she hobbled and picketed them. The camp was in a big basin with a creek running through it. Cherie started to make a fire and then supper. Cherie and Jen both love to sleep out under the stars; she said they just put down one of the mantles then laid down some horse blankets and put down their sleeping bags and threw other mantles on top. It works great unless it's a real downpour.

She and Jen had spent many good nights out under the stars talking and watching the satellites go across the sky or a falling star until they fell asleep. The clients that they had were from Holland, and they wanted to see snow and grizzly bears. Cherie said she thought they could show them both.

On the second day, they took them over to another ridge they called the birds' nest; that is where they saw the majority of the grizzly bears. They had nearly completed the trip up there when they found a big patch of snow below them. Cherie told them she might be able to find another patch that they could play in; then as she was watching the snow, she thought she saw something move.

She got out her field glasses and—lo and behold—if it wasn't a sow grizzly bear with two cubs. She was lifting her head to smell the air; she had obviously gotten their scent. She and her cubs were having a cool nap on the snow on a hot July day. They got some good pictures and were very happy customers. She got back to camp to make a good supper and sit around the fire and tell stories. It looked like there was a good chance that it was going to rain that night.

Jen and Cherie found a tarp in the old cabin. It was one that had the rubber covering on one side. They threw that over themselves and called the dogs in under with them and went to sleep. In the wee hours of the morning, the three border collies went flying out from under the tarp and took off barking at something. Cherie started yelling at them to come back as she feared it might be a porcupine, and she sure didn't need something like that to happen.

The next morning, she was thinking what it might have been and thought, whatever it was, I bet it got the shit scared out of her. She said, "Can you imagine some animal sneaking up on this big silver thing, and three noisy black-and-white things come flying out from under it. It would scare the hell out of me."

Jen and Cherie were just packing up the last horse when one of the guys came and said, "We have a bear in camp." Cherie thought, *Oh yeah, OK,* thinking it was at the other end of the meadow.

He was persistent and said she might want to come and see, so she did, and sure enough, it was a grizzly bear, and it was very close—just on the other side of the creek. The first thing she did was tell the dogs to lie down. Then she yelled at it and whistled really loud. It just looked up at her and started to come toward her. Then she stepped out into the open where it was sure to see her, and she yelled and whistled really loud and waved her arms. This time it saw her and took off like a flash. She said it made her wonder if that was what was sneaking around in the wee hours of the morning. She said, "We have had several different experiences in these mountains with grizzly bears, and all have been pleasant. I hope it always stays that way."

CHAPTER 9

The Trip up Top: In Search of Twin Lakes with Jennifer
by Cherie Jackson

In 1998, I was still married to Darcy Jackson, the father of my children. We used to take riding adventures too. The plan was made; we were heading in for a longer trip and hoped to find Twin Lakes this time.

We decided to go for four days this time, and we had three pack horses with us, and Christina, a friend from Horsefly, came with us. We already knew the trail and had little trouble, except for a few stubborn mules that wanted to lie down with the packs on. We'd heard there was a trail off the end of the airport by Silvertip Lodge that headed up through the barn to the alpine, and our goal was to find it and make it this time. We found it, but there was a lot of trail-cutting to be done as, over the years, many trees had fallen down. We cleared trail all day and still never made it to the top. We finally came across a suitable spot to camp on the side of that mountain, calling it Last Chance Camp and unpacked the horses and made some supper. It was all worth it. The next day, the view was absolutely breathtaking. All the various rock formations were amazing.

Once we got to the alpine, we had a better idea of the lay of the land and decided to ride toward Hobson Lake. As we picked our way along the bottom of an inviting but daunting ridge, we wondered what was on the other side—perhaps Twin Lakes?

Before long, Hobson Lake came into view. I still remember that awesome feeling at the splendour that was before us. Hobson Lake was even more beautiful from above. Its amazing turquoise color stuck out like the most dazzling diamond with the rocky peaks as her setting. The alpine meadows above her were scattered with a myriad of wildflowers. We made our way to the end of the ridge and up to the highest vantage point. We left the horses on a patch of snow and climbed up on this little plateau. Just when we thought the view couldn't get any better, we were delighted once again as we could see the Clearwater River winding down a valley and the estuary it created as it flowed into Hobson Lake, and all this surrounded by those amazing mountains. What lucky souls we are to be able to experience such a view and right in our backyard.

In July, we were ready to do another trip in search of Twin Lakes. We would have liked to have more time but could only spend four days. With the trail all cut out around the end of the east arm and up the mountain to the alpine, we were pretty sure it would happen this time. On a trip like this, it is never hard to find someone who wants to tag along, so we took a couple of friends with us and also decided to take Jen and Jason along on this trip. Jen was eleven, and Jason was nine—and let's face it, after Jen had a taste of the high country, there was no leaving her behind anymore, which was fine with us as she was a help, not a hindrance, and we knew Jason would be the same. Once we reached the alpine, this time, instead of riding along the ridge over to Hobson Lake, we decided to take a left and tried to make our way around the end of it. We could see once we got there what the options were. Let me tell you, it is always steeper than it looks, but we threw fear to the wind, and before we knew it, we were on the top of that ridge overlooking Twin Lakes with the glacier behind it. *Wow!* It was worth the climb and so very beautiful. It was as the story was told—the two lakes were very close together, each flowing into a different valley. All we had to do was make it down to them.

We were having a break before heading down when we came across a hole in the mountain. We threw rocks into it but could not hear them hit the bottom. So what was it, a natural vent of some kind? It was a little spooky. I remembered we were all gathered around in a circle, holding on to our horses, and we all just backed away, not sure what we had found. The way off the mountain was so treacherous and hard on the horses because of all the snow that was mixed with the rock. But we made it down, vowing to find a better way down on the way home. It was seven thirty when we got off that portion of the ridge, and we finally made camp at nine thirty that night. We had done it. We finally made it to Twin Lakes, and the kids were there to share the experience.

The next morning, as I sat looking at the countryside, I wondered what was beyond that glacier. We had heard of an old mining camp on one of the rivers that flowed into the Clearwater. More adventures and exploration awaited us. We rode over toward the river, hoping to find the way down and to explore our options for finding the gold-mining camp, but there was no fast way down, so we decided it would have to wait for another day.

As we drew near the crossover spot, we found that there was a lot of snow and some glacial ice as well, and right near the top, there was a corona that we had to climb over. I wanted nothing to do with this experience. What was that I said about throwing fear to the wind? It was a bit too risky for me, especially since I had the kids with me.

Darcy climbed up on foot and took a look and skied back down on his cowboy boots. He figured we could make it. In my mind, I was still trying to figure out how I was going to get out of this. Poor Jason was chucking his cookies. His nerves were getting the best of him, and Jen didn't want anything to do with it either, but Darcy said, "It's do or die," so off we went.

I'm going to say that the grade of the climb was nearly 70 percent. We had to run up, leading the horses as they were lunging up behind us, and as I ran, my knees were hitting the snow. Let me tell you, there was no room for error—one bad move and we both would be doing endos down the mountain. The guys went first, and then Christina, I, and Darcy brought the kids and the horses up one at a time. I called this experience suicide climb on a toenail ridge. It was a rush, but I had no intention of ever doing it again. At the time, I thought I would never experience anything so scary yet exhilarating again. I have since changed my mind and have a much greater understanding of what a great mountain horse can do.

CHAPTER 10

Stu and Cherie usually do a trail ride for the Canim Lake Indian band every year. Sometimes they split into two groups of ten or twelve people in a group. That is when you all pray for good weather. But as they have found out, it does not always work out.

A perfect sunny day and a great ride for most of these clients.

Cherie picking huckleberries for pancakes in the morning.

Cherie sitting by a mountain fireplace.

A bunch of dudes getting ready to go on a trail ride.

They will be going up Bosk Mountain above the lodge. For some, it will be their first trail ride. To look down on the world from up Bosk Mountain is a wonderful sight and experience.

Since I have sold the ranch and am retired to fishing and telling stories, I still dream of just maybe getting me a nice ram someday, but dreaming is free, so I just might do a lot of dreaming. Just maybe, someday, I will talk Stu into taking me on a sheep hunt.

Cherie, with all her love for the outdoors and mountains, really is not a hunter at heart; she really does not like to shoot anything unless it is absolutely necessary, but being in the business that they are in, hunting is a very important part of their business.

Stuart has exclusive guiding rights to three thousand five hundred square miles of prime big-game country bordering and inside of Wells Gray Provincial Park; their territory is located in Management Units 5-2, 5-15, and 3-46, and includes a portion of the remote Cariboo Mountains Provincial Park and a portion of Wells Gray Park. The terrain varies from slow meandering rivers, where the great chinook and sockeye salmon spawn, to lofty alpine meadows and mountains reaching up to ten thousand feet. Over a third of the area is wilderness without roads, with the remainder having logging road access to their camps and hot spots for moose, deer, cougar, and bear. Cherie has covered most every part of this area and a good portion on horseback.

CHAPTER 11

Spring bear hunts really get the adrenaline flowing, especially when they get a nice big grizzly bear, like the one Thomas Berntsson from Sweden got—he measured nine foot six with a skull measurement of twenty-five and three quarters. They used dogs to track him; their dogman was Steve Mohr, and he is really good at it. Clark Stewart, from Charlotte, North Carolina—with his fifteen-plus-inch Boone and Crockett cat—can kind of turn you on too.

Then there is the time when Dylan, the guide, took a hunter up the Niagara valley. They shot a really nice bull moose late in the evening; after field-dressing the moose, they left it there and walked back to camp. The plan was that they would go back in the morning and pack it out with the horses. But during the night, a grizzly bear sniffed out the kill and said, "Thank you for leaving me this nice moose supper." He ate one hind quarter and up the side to the front shoulder, then he ate the entire gut pile. Cherie said that was an easy moose to pack out.

A hunter's moose that a grizzly bear had supper off.

The grizzly bear will sometimes cover the rest of the moose with dirt, grass, and sticks so he can come back later and feed on it. However, on this particular time, he must have been pleasantly stuffed and didn't feel up to covering it, so all was not wasted.

They don't seem to have fear of the human scent and will, on some occasions, be there as soon as the kill is made. Those of us who have done a lot of hunting in a grizzly-bear country sometimes refer to the shot as ringing the dinner bell for the grizzly bears. It is amazing just how much these bears can pack. I have had them pack a young bull elk up a mountainside into the alders on a slide and then cover it. When one approaches a kill like this, they should only do it with an experienced hunter or guide because that bear will guard that kill with his life. These critters are very unpredictable; a mother with cubs is one to give a wide berth to. The other time is when a boar is partnered up with a sow that is in estrus. They demand and should be given the outmost respect.

CHAPTER 12

A Trip to Africa: The Realization of a Dream as told by Cherie Jackson

"For us, a trip to Africa was always one of those 'Wouldn't it be nice? Can you imagine?' It was always in the back of our minds that someday we would go. Well, I guess all that positive energy and thinking finally paid off."

In April of 2010, they bought a hunt that was auctioned off by GOABC, which was generously donated by Matt and Sylvia Greeff from Africa. The trip was a ten-day plains game hunt, and Big 5 Photo Safari, which included impala, blesbok, red hartebeest, and one blue or black wildebeest, and one nonhunter could go along.

Stu and Cherie, standing on the plains of South Africa, ready for whatever challenges that await them.

She said that Matt and Sylvia, along with their two daughters, Amber and Savannah, made them feel so welcome, providing for them right down to the smallest details. And being that Cherie and Stuart are outfitters themselves, they really could appreciate that. Matt asked them if they would like to go into an exclusive hunting concession he had just gotten in the Loskop Dam Nature Reserve. He felt that they would have a good opportunity to take a great kudu, as well as a zebra and an impala, which were all on their list. He did warn them that they would be sleeping in a bush camp in tents. Cherie said she thought it would be fun to have the ultimate African experience, tenting in the wilds of Africa.

The night sounds are quite different than what she had been used to in the mountains of British Columbia. She said when the lions roared at night, it was scary, but it was an incredible sound. She said the hyenas are really eerie and the dingoes are somewhat like our coyotes. She missed her horses but could see that they would never be practical because the lions and the panthers would be hunting them all the time. Besides that, they could cover so much more ground with their four-wheel-drive vehicles.

The Loskop Dam Nature Reserve did not disappoint them. The number of different game that they saw there was amazing; they saw seven rhinos in one bunch, herds of zebras, wildebeest, cape buffalo, sables, impala, water buck, eland, nyala, and hippos and crocodiles in the Olifants River. They went fishing for barbel, or catfish as we know it; from there, they were able to see giraffes and kudu as well.

Stu took a nice kudu, fifty-eight and a half inches, a zebra, black wildebeest, and a springbuck. They took excellent care of their trophies for Stu and Cherie; they dipped them, packed them, and shipped them home for them to take to the taxidermy. When they were finished, they would be put in their new lodge on the Horsefly River with Stu's many other trophies.

Stu said, "I got him," and Cherie was proud of her man. He is a good shot, but that is what he does for a living; he took five animals and got them all with the first shot.

She said they saw many different animals in their natural habitat, and it was very interesting to see a giraffe with that long neck, but when you realize what they eat, you very well can understand why they need that long neck. They get most of their food from the tops of the trees, and when their heads are on the same level as the tops of the tress, they can look down and see a lot better if there should be some predator trying to sneak up on them.

The country was a lot different than in British Columbia. You didn't have the wild-running mountain streams and rivers, and the mountains were not so rugged and steep with all those snowcaps. There were no big fir, spruce, or pine trees. The air was not as fresh and crisp in the mornings, but then, it was warmer too. She said, "I missed my horses. There is just nothing more beautiful than seeing a string of pack horses meandering across the valley floor with all those big snow-covered mountains in the background. The lakes are so much more vibrant and fresh-looking, where in Africa, they are more stagnant. But we don't have hippos and crocodiles, so when you take that all into consideration, everything kind of fits—after all, we were nearly half a world away from my beautiful British Columbia. But we enjoyed it, and would we do it again? Yes, we would love to.

"There is so much to see and learn about the animals and their habitat. The hippos that are in the lakes and rivers stay nearly submerged, and if you get too close to them, you could be asking for trouble. The crocodile is always looking for an easy meal, and if you are in a canoe and get too close, he could look at you as lunch. Some of them are real big, but most of the time, they just slither into the water. The water buffalo is an animal that looks at you as if he would like to charge at you, and they will if you give them a chance. The rhino is an animal that can do your vehicle a lot of damage, if he makes his mind too, but like most times, he will run into the bush if he is given the opportunity. I had no knowledge of what to expect of them, so I listened very closely to our guide. The lion is such a laid-back big cat, and most of the time you see them, they are just lying in the shade, but if they are on the hunt, you don't want to stray too far from your vehicle. The panther is a night animal, so you don't see him too much, but you hear him in the night, and he gives you the feeling he could be stalking you at any time. Like the roar of the lion, it certainly is intimidating, and you know why he is called the king of the jungle. When he roars, some of the smaller animals get excited and run, and the females will intercept them and make the kill. Most of the killing is done by the females."

This critter's front legs are too long for his neck, so he gets into an awkward stance to get a drink and hopes the lion isn't lurking too close to the water hole.

These buffalo are taking advantage of the shade that the trees are providing for them. The white birds help to keep the flies in check.

A kudu at a drinking hole.

What are you doing in my world? Are you dangerous?

Cherie sitting at the back. She said, "I sure hope these critters don't buck because it's a long way to the ground, and this is not a bronco saddle by any means."

Now that I was getting the hang of it, we were off into the bushes of Africa to see what we could find. You're sure to get an awesome view from being up so high.

Mr. Opportunist lying in the shade, waiting for a feline or a spring buck to come along—he will take whichever comes first.

After the hunt, they toured around parts of Africa; they visited Cape Town and then the famous Victoria Falls. Cherie got to ride an elephant, and it would reach back with its trunk, and you could give it a peanut. She said that when you lead them around, they would look for a peanut and would fish it right out of your hand with the tip of their trunk.

There sure are a lot of people that live way down there. Stu and a friend doing some sightseeing from Table Mountain, looking down on Cape Town.

So this is where and how they grow. Boy, the ripe ones sure do taste good too. It was surprising to see that bananas grew up. You would expect them to hang down.

The Victoria Falls were a spectacular sight to see; they are so big and intimidating. The mist or spray covered a big area around the falls and was like a light rain that your hair and clothes would get damp in no time. The vegetation looked like the sprinklers were running twenty-four seven, and I guess in a way, they were.

The Victoria Falls! What a sight to see. The spray makes you feel like you are in a light rain.

Cherie rewarding the elephant with a peanut while sitting on its knee. She went for a ride on him later and said as long as you kept feeding him peanuts, he would do most anything for you.

African landscape.

Cherie says, "Beautiful? Yes, in its own way, but it can't compare with my beautiful British Columbia. Those snowcapped mountains, the forest with all those big conifers, and the rivers and lakes so clear and blue will always be so dear to my heart. To just ride my horse over the mountain trails and cross the rivers that run so clear is what charges my batteries and keeps me going. To see all this is like being in a new world, but really, it's not. The Creator sure had an awful good imagination when he put this world all together, and everything fits so well and is so very much alive. To me, this country looks much older than British Columbia. It looks old and worn down compared to British Columbia. But who knows? Maybe the Creator practiced here first."

*   *   *

Yes, it no doubt was a trip of a lifetime for them, and would I want to do it? *Yes,* I would have jumped at a chance to go and experience what she did. But I must admit, I was glad to see her back at the lodge, knowing she was all safe and well. What wonderful memories those trophies and pictures will bring to her and Stu in the coming years. But for now, she will keep making those delicious meals that everyone loves. And because of the strong love she has for the outdoors, only the shadow knows the trails she will continue to blaze.

In 2010, Stu and Cherie decided to build a new house on the Horsefly River. It has a spectacular view, and when they are finished, it will be a hand on satisfaction, knowing that they had picked the logs for a special reason. All those logs and beams were sanded by her, and they designed it their way. What an accomplishment it will be.

I watched that little beaver peeling logs so that the carpenters wouldn't be held up when they came to do some other framing. I saw her sanding and varathaning logs up on a ladder so high that only very skilled workman would do. One day Gloria and I went to see how the new house was coming, and here she was, moving drain rock around the house with a wheelbarrow so that the machine that was going to do the backfilling would not have to stand and wait. I guess the guys that were supposed to have done it thought that it was a little too much work.

I hope they don't leave it too long before they sit back and enjoy it. Time stops for no one, and all too soon, we realize there is only one inch left on the ruler of life. I would have liked to put a few trophy heads in their lodge, but I have left that a little too long, unless Stuart would let me put a fish in it. It will be so good to go there just to sit and listen to her and her group play and sing and entertain us. I can hardly wait for Christmas next year; it will be a special gathering at their house. In 2011, we were all given a pleasant surprise when Ty and Jen announced that they were getting married. He had proposed to her while they were riding home from a long, hard day of working cattle on the range. As he rode his horse up close to her so that he could reach out and put his arm around her, he said, "Jen, would you marry me?" She was so excited; she tried to reach out to kiss him, and on a walking horse that is not the easiest thing to do. So she said, "Why don't we stop and do that again?"

It wasn't long before they made their announcement to everyone. And for Cherie and Stu, they were so excited they didn't know where to start first. Jen is so much like her mom in so many ways; the apple didn't fall too far from the tree with that one. It was one of the most different weddings that I have ever attended. It was done in a complete Western style from beginning to end.

Jen and Ty really did plan their wedding together, and it resulted in a perfect day. They used a Quonset on the ranch for their reception. All along the inside of the building, they built a corral of rustic planks, and behind those planks, they lined the walls with small poplar and birch trees with the leaves in all their splendid autumn colors. Spaced into that were small spruce trees. They covered the floor with shavings, and on that, they set tables and chairs for two hundred people. As they entered the Quonset, they had an arch that the bride and groom would walk through on their way to the head table; the table was set on a raised platform, and in front of that was a dance floor. Everything was decorated in a country Western flair: hay bales, flowers, and pumpkins. The whole inside of the building was lit up with strings of small white lights.

The ceremony was held in the middle of a large hayfield. It gave the guests a spectacular view of the mountains at the far end of the valley, surrounded on each side by ridges of high hills and round bales in the field. Darcy had made an arch out of horseshoes that he had painted black. It had a romantic style to it, and the horseshoes were purposely set in an upward position to catch good fortune. It was placed at the end of the aisle, where it would frame the wedding ceremony. They had decorated with sunflowers, hay bales, cream cans filled with bulrushes, and fall flowers and grasses that Cherie and Jennifer had collected.

On each side of the arch, they had a hitching rail for the best men and groom to tie their horses when they rode in for the ceremony. The bridesmaids were brought in on an old-fashioned wagon, and the bride arrived in a fancy carriage that her father drove. After the vows, the bride, with her long dress and all, got onto the back of the horse that her husband was riding, and they rode off together to take pictures among the hay bales that were still out in the field.

The entire community had pitched in to make it such a memorable day, something that happens when living in small rural communities. It was wonderful.

When I look back thirty-five years ago, on that same property, there were two little girls that were helping me tag and vaccinate calves, and Cherie was one of them; and now, she was watching her daughter getting married on that same place. Whether she thought about it or not, her daughter was following a trail that she had blazed through life. Now they were ready to start on a new trail with a whole new set of plans. One never knows all who might be following our trail, so best we keep it as straight as possible.

Cherie's (and Darcy Jackson's) son, Jason, is an equally impressive and very special individual. Like all young boys, he liked his cars and girls and did his thing while growing up. Then he went to Northern Alberta to make his mark in the oil patch, and he has done very well for himself. It wasn't long before he got himself a nice pickup and had a little jingle in his pocket. Then one day, he brought home a girlfriend, and we all really liked her. Sarah is a very special lady, and we love her very much; together they make a very nice couple.

Sarah is an accountant and has a very responsible job but enjoys getting out there in the dirt to quad and work on Jason's old cars with him. While she is beautiful and fun, she has a great sense of responsibility and a sense of direction in life. They have bought their own home, which is beautiful and has a big fenced backyard perfect for kids. They are both great with kids and will make wonderful parents one day.

During the spring of 2012, Jason and Sarah came home to visit. Jason had a big secret, and he wanted to find the perfect moment to reveal it. He took Sarah up to Horsefly Falls and proposed to her; of course, she said yes, and he gave her a beautiful ring. We were all so happy for them and so happy that Jason had found such a wonderful person to share his life with.

They are both deeply rooted in country, and when Jason and Sarah got married, they too had their wedding outside on a ranch here in Horsefly. They came back to Jason's hometown to get married, which was a very special thing to do.

They chose to get married at a local venue owned by friends of everyone involved in the wedding. Franz and Sylvia Laffer and their great family cater to weddings at Sunshine Ranch. They no longer use their barn as a barn and have decorated it up and rent it out for weddings. They have a beautiful yard and have various places where you can set up an altar, where the couple can exchange their vows while their friends and guests sit on bales to watch and take pictures. Sarah had their wedding organized to the last detail, and everything went off smoothly.

Being that Jason and Sarah share an interest in old cars, they used an old muscle car that Jason has restored for the bride to drive herself and her attendants to the wedding site in. The groom and best men came in on an old Chevy pickup that has been restored.

We all watched anxiously as a wild thunder and lightning storm moved closer and closer, wondering if the whole wedding would get rained on. It dropped a few sprinkles but nothing significant. At the last minute, the storm split and went around Sunshine Ranch, the sun shone, and the ceremony was beautiful. I'd say their wedding was blessed by the gods!

Cherie is very proud of her children. I know Grandma and Grandpa sure are. It goes to show that precious flowers just need to be nourished and protected and allowed to grow strong. It has been so good to see her children make wise choices, and yes, Cherie has played a big part in it, but a good portion of the credit goes to Darcy as well.

I attempt to finish this as I sit at her table, looking out the window that gives one an excellent view of the Horsefly River and the valley that takes care of all the watershed of those big snowcapped mountains she so dearly loves. As I sit here, I can look down the Horsefly River and watch the bald eagles less than a hundred yards from the lodge fight over the scraps of Stuart's trapping.

At times there are six or more jockeying for position to get to the biggest pile of scraps. We see the moose and coyotes and tracks of wolves and foxes and all the critters that are too shy to venture out in the daylight. The bird feeders are always entertaining as there is an assortment of birds there all the time.

The reason I am here is that my wife, Gloria, and I are house-sitting while Cherie and Stuart are away. This house is built with a hunter trapper in mind; every window gives you a great view, and as we slept in their bed, we could look out the window as we hunkered down under the covers and saw the stars and the moon shining. That room was, no doubt, built with that in mind as they both love to sleep out under the stars.

ABOUT THE AUTHOR

Lloyd is a man filled with courage and determination. He is never one to believe that the job is too big and can't be done. If he himself can't get it done, he will find someone who can help him to achieve his goal. Today he has mellowed some but still is a very determined man. His daughter, Cherie, is very much like him, so is it any wonder that he would write a book about her? She is a trailblazer who shares his determination and love for the mountains.

His honest, heartfelt writing style will hold your interest to the very last page and make you want to read it again for a second time.

Edwards Brothers Malloy
Thorofare, NJ USA
June 6, 2014